LOVE BITES

BY ELLIE SPARKS

© Ellie Sparks 2025 Portsmouth

All rights reserved. No part of this book may be reproduced or modified in any form, including photocopying, recording, or by any information storage and retrieval system, without permission in writing from the publisher.

For You, Mum. I Love You.

~ *Dead In The Water* ~

I'm all used up,
darling boy,
and my gelatine
organs are splayed
all over our
bedroom carpet.
How many times
do you have to
massacre
my devotion,
depict me as the
cerulean target?
I came here with
the intention of
declaring,
and all I'm issued
is a seminar
in despairing.
What does a girl
do when her
ability to
L o V e
is choking?
I guess I'll just
lie down in the
stream out back,
crepuscular,
carnivorous,
croaking.

~ *If Only I Could* Gut *You* ~

My heart
is woven into
your sleeve, guts
spewing
everywhere.
You carry this
grit with you,
this gaping organ,
hoping you'll
be spared.
There is no
redemption for a
truant who crunches
into aortic
chambers.
There is no
forgiveness for a
guy who thieves
rotting limbs
for his own
pleasure.
If only I could
g u t
you, rid you
from this lifeline,
but I'm appended
to your cotton
v-neck, left
decomposing
deathly.

A victim
of your cratered
time.

~ Horror Show ~

I've been breaking
the eggshells
of our masochistic
love, the living room
light flickering
over the adversity.
Why is it you
always make me
into the bad guy,
the titanic judge
of your self-fed
atrophy?
I've glazed gasoline
over this horror show,
bleeding whatever
hope I can just to
ruin your anatomy.
I just plead, once
your organs start
flailing, I can
flee from this
barbarity, grasp
my limbs before the
battery, live life
more naturally.
In your death,
I'll give you the
greatest flattery.
After all, wasn't
linking me with the

hive of your lore
your grandest
strategy?

~ Fifteen Seconds ~

I've been naming
your freckles beneath
corrosive starlight,
yet you say you've
enshrouded their
names.
*I wonder: will one day
you forget mine?
Have we purged
our fifteen seconds
of fame?*

~ Teenage Fantasy ~

We are crushed velvet.
A delicacy
brimming from
hushed regality.
This armour
softens our fall,
and these secrets
veneer our
fallacy.
With rumours
spreading
like undertones, this
orchestra
reaps our divine
balladry.
If only existence
was as core-clapping
as this
feral
fantasy.

~ Novocaine ~

I swallow the
thunder,
and bite my lip
to contain the
hurricane.
How is it
every time I'm
with you I feel
like I'm nibbling
on novocaine?
I could create a
treehouse from
my tragedy,
sputter up my
scars, and you'd
still laugh at
my pain.
How does a girl
disembowel
her own gullet?
All you do
is cough up
rain.

~ Succubus ~

Is she prettier
than she was on
Bumble - a
pouty petunia, all
lip filler and no
empathy?
Why is it that girls
like this always
arch and
crater
me?
Does she make
you shitty playlists -
generic songs from
the 90s,
claiming these
are her
heartbreak
history?
I was birthed back
then and I don't
let narcissism
snatch the brunt
of me.
Does she fill
your mug with
curling espresso,
wake up, make
B&B and clean?
Come on, love.

Can't you see?
She's a
Succubus
feeding on
your
apathy.
*So much for
your
artful
trophy...*

~ Sordid History ~

I know it won't work
but, still,
I sit here plucking
lesions from
my collarbone,
trying to recall all
the times you
were *good* to me.
Turns out your
mind loads
blanks when it
fails to romanticise
a sordid history.
I thought our
toxins would
bubble over
once we both
asserted we'd
never leave.
Guess I never
really swallowed
the rancid stench
of situational
irony.

~ Dead On The Interstate ~

I burned my tongue
on your homicide.
Found myself
gutted on the freeway.
Why is it
every
celestial dawn
I dowse my bones
in doomsday?
I purged my
paralysis
as you glided
down the
runway.
How could you
twist my
innards idle,
disrepair me
this way?

~ Gone Girl ~

I've been trying
to decipher
why you
annihilated
me
the way you did,
but all I can
speculate is you
were
parched for
fresh
blood.
You always
accursed your
mutual absorption an
unattainable bid,
threaded
barbed wire
around your
affection.
I guess there's
too much carnage
burning out here,
tying treason
around this
ailing love.
I guess it's time
to puke this
melancholy
and give up.

After all, how long
does it take
a girl to
disappear?

~ Rib Eye Steak ~

I am a crime scene
and you cleaned up
poorly -
left my entrails swimming
in acaricide, heart
tainted by sin.
Was I just a product
of the prize-winning,
the rib eye steak of
an initiation ritual,
your means to begin?
If I'm to die out then,
eat extinction,
breathe the bloodiest
fiction, I'll just
chew the crust
of your chest
for a try.
These cavernous
catacombs
never dealt me an
equitable hand, never
queried the pendulum,
let me cradle a
varicose life.
All I wanted was to
fade into the
cobalt ether
and fly...
Instead, I'm limbless

on the kitchen floor,
ribcage collateral
damage from your
flesher's knife.
So much for
finding a guy
I could scribe
literatim...

~ Bloodlust / Curling Marshes ~

It's more radical
than swimming -
this tidal wave
of bloodlust,
seeping carnage over our
marital bed.
How is it I buried
my seething
in my intestines,
cradled ratsbane
after we wed?
I'm repressing
all the hypotheses
you clamped
to my
ailing head.
Sometimes I
peruse these
curling marshes,
muse if I'd be
better off
dead.

~ Sticky Treason ~

You adorn
adulterous lips
and every time I
kiss you,
I have to hold
my breath.
Your persecution
reeks of duplicity
and as I
hug your bones
I lick the
lifelessness
that's left.
I'm sick of
painting plagues
and committing crimes
and murdering
this mess.
I am repressing
the time,
the stains,
the eons I
wasted
to impress...

~ *The Monarch And The Butcherer* ~

The ache...
Why won't it
go away?
There are innards
caressing the walls,
phantoms stalking
my reveries.
Why did I ever
believe
we could work?
A monarch and
a butcherer.
The accused and the
hunter.
I can only depict
this paralysis in
verse.
So there, I guess this
is the reckoning.
My shackled winter.
What would you
remark if I told you
I feel like a
fraudulent writer?
How would you
concoct my
cryptic curse?
After all this,
I'm just
a mannequin, and

you're the
maker.
We're going to
spew into cloudburst.
Of both of us,
I guess I was
always the griever.
Now you can
dub me your
severed.

~ What If I Am
The Crime Scene? ~

I weave my doting
into diction
but my vowels
no longer rhyme.
I guess when your
chest coughs
cartilage confetti,
you start to feel like
his crime.
I gouge one
eye stoic, and the
other crimson.
Sporting vicissitude
has become my
favourite
past-time.
I guess I should be
seething,
running, undoing
my own extinction.
Berating myself
for bypassing
those signs...
I guess, then,
we were the most
crestfallen fiction.
Even from the eruption,
you were never
mine.

I guess the animation
will return to me...
Ravage me...
Encase me...
S o m e t i m e.

~ Death's Door ~

I've beckoned
the vultures
to drag my stale,
stiff, velveteen
corpse away.
You've left me
caked in gravel,
like your
cremated promises,
forsaken on the
front walkway.
I'd rather by
asphyxiated in soot,
skin rubbed,
crusted,
crimped and
frayed.
I'd rather they exile
me anywhere
but *here,*
so I can tackle the
clogging of my
airways.

~ *Stop Torching My Poetry* ~

The last text
you sent me was
drunk with expletives,
paralytic with
expired romances.
Why are you still
torching
my poetry,
dyeing our
memories in
domestic stresses?
I don't know
how many times
I can hang from
these ivy-tipped
tresses, overhear
familial blessings.
This ecstasy
didn't blossom,
just stripped me
of my sterling.
Will I one day
let this mauling
lie, stop sucking
the poison from
this purging?
I guess this
tempest
is still
gurgling.

~ Slaughterhouse Cries ~

The loathing persists,
but so do I -
rocking near
the mantle
with bloodshot
eyes.
I don't know how
you fathom
malting your
Freudian lies,
persisting as an
archetype of
a distorted
disguise.
I wonder
wistfully
If I can outrun
your spies, yank out
this rancidity,
coruscate
wine-glass
wise.
But you pin
me there, skin
sodden, exhaling
slaughterhouse cries,
and you turn my
treason
tepid
until this

bloodshed
dries.

~ Hoax ~

Chainsaw it all -
every utterance
I ever croaked.
Your spite is
sprouting fangs.
My poetry is
your hoax.
I guess we'll
all preach I'm the
victor-turned-venom
trope.
My voice box is
eliminated by
your axe, inhaling
the end because
I ever
spoke.

~ *You. Are. My. End.* ~

Your words
trail behind
like lost ghosts…
Apparitions fluttered
off the Richter scale,
straight into the
abyss.
Do you know
exactly how you
decimate
me when you
tug on my longing
like this?
If I am to always
be so enamoured
by ailment,
can you at least
not erect me
a frostbitten flame?
I'm stumbling stiff,
stitching loose lips,
falling victim
to your
macabre games...
Does every
adoration
bleed blame,
bathe shame,
incise the same?
I guess you're my end,

and I'm the
protagonist,
slain.

~ *Pesty Pendulum* ~

I keep treading
carefully
around the mines you've
soldered into your soul.
I've used my compass,
I've consulted my
swinging pendulum,
but I still
can't unearth you.
Are you still adrift
in the Everglades?
Are you still embracing
hypothermia, slumbering
anaesthetised beneath
glaciated
embers?

~ Angry Abattoir ~

The ache is
an abattoir.
A shambles
stuttering in my
sternum.
Maybe you shouldn't
have mangled
our bruise.
I guess you
could say
my limbs are
gradually learning
what fluids fluctuate
when the plasma
starts to ooze,
what to do when
the combat
is returning,
how to exist
like hacking
is
a
rouse.
How do I abandon
the lashing of you?

~ *Perishing In Kyoto* ~

Midnight catches
on the water,
and cobalt indigo
ripples in slumber.
I stroke silken iris
stamens, stumbling into
our dissociating
disencumber.
How did I end up
teething on your
Trojan thunder,
catching on koi
before ambling and
anchoring under?
I just can't comprehend
why you wintered
our Kyoto-clambering
summer, these
temple tours and
Polaroid plains,
campfire fables littered
with sagacious wonder.
Have you snipped
the chord of us,
drained these
dreamscapes of
calligraphy, of chastity,
of artistry,
of *colour?*
I guess I'll just

stare at my reflection
in this iodine-inked
ryokan pond
until my sanctity ebbs,
flurries, flakes
and recovers.

~ Bludgeoned Romeo ~

We wash ashore
like body parts
on the
Californian
coast.
I keep asking
myself if this
craving I cloak
over your limbs
is me coveting
your ghost.
If you would
evanesce for me,
where did you go?
I guess, after
all this time,
you really are
my
bludgeoned
Romeo.

~ Pity Party ~

I'm on heartache
boulevard
and you don't dare
show up for the
pity party.
I've been hugging
my own failure,
aching for your
jousting to bleed
into anarchy.
Who am I if not
a mattress-hopper,
a soul-scalper,
a spearhead of
seared
sanity?
I'll keep on watching
the warped waves,
festering in the
memory of your
false
flattery.

~ I'm The Best Motion Picture ~

You call me a
horror movie, but you
have no clue
what slashing
I can unleash.
I have experience of
grinding human flesh
between my
turpentine
teeth.
On the weekend,
I brand a machete
in my martyr's grip.
I forage through
undergrowth until
I let rage slip.
And when you dare
feast me to the
coyotes, I'll lure
you to the grave.
Seduce your
cratered spirit
with my
bloodthirsty stave.
So don't tell me
I'm a terror movie,
because I already
know.
Now, do you want
me to grant you

a dutiful
deathblow?

~ Hot Death ~

The planets align
silently
and we flatline
into ruin
like
an old Sedan
at the junkyard.
Why is it we
f r a c t u r e
this time
every evening?
Half-hearted
phone conversations
are starting to
sound like
elevator music.
Your groans are
perspiring like my
pores, marinating my
tolerance with
hot
death.
As the planets align,
we disorient,
detach,
decompose.
Why is it I barely
feel like I know
you now?
This eroding

attachment
is the cruellest way
to expire.

~ Icarus Can't Save Us Now ~

I keep my wounds
closer
than I keep you,
and perhaps that's
why we leaked
incision.
Else, maybe that's
why the silver-tipped
ether we
fell
through.
Maybe the only way
to pin my heart
is to devote
my bones to this
electric blue,
preserve the Pegasus
through which this
Icarus-lit sky
we flew to.

~ The Reaper's Call ~

There was poison
in the flowers
you gifted me,
and arsenic in my
arsenal.
Why are you always
raving to
execute me,
host a party
at my funeral?
If I'm mere
permanence,
a depiction of
redemption,
why am I always
hearing the
Reaper's call?
I don't quite
understand
how I can go from
a *lover* to
a *sinner* to
a *morality rule.*

~ We Can't Say We Weren't Told ~

It's almost as if
they tried to warn us.
The sun burns
black
when it tastes
our love.
The sea sears to
ash
when it inhales
our pestilence.
The ether malts
maroon
when it cradles our
calamity.
We are not made
for any type of
terrain,
any balance of Themis,
any palace or
poverty.
The downpour
will always
siphon us
parched.

~ Pretty Epitaph ~

What doesn't kill
you
makes you wish
you were dead.
I wish you'd stop
stapling epiphany
to my
shotgun
head.
You know I'm just
going to
bite the bullet and
swallow the led.
Why don't you
craft me
a pretty epitaph
instead?

~ Ceremony Of Corpses ~

We're having our
honeymoon in a
graveyard
and our reception
in a morgue.
I won't chew your
limbs off
until I've tasted dawn.
And yes, maybe I
set this up so
we would never see
light of day.
You brought your
skeletons to the
ceremony
anyway.

~ *Songbird Unheard* ~

All I do is bleed.
All you see are words.
Perhaps I am not
the prologue, but the
cat-eyed hook on
the blurb.
I always hoped I could
hex you through
my soliloquies
like a beseeching,
valiant songbird.
Alas, my elegies
turn to eulogies
and my stanzas
weep unheard.

~ A Belly Full Of Death ~

There are still
coffee stains
on your nightstand
and teardrops
of cologne
on your plush pillows.
If I am the one
rotting in reverie,
why are you not
wilting like a willow?
I've tried trimming
the Polaroids and
shredding the
ticket stubs,
but you're still
prying, like a brandishing
in my psyche,
chewing on my chest
with your
cerulean
love.
How does a girl
behead desire
when it is bloated
in her own belly?
Will she forever be
haunted by the spectre
she bled for
when she was
just twenty?

I guess the route
to freedom
is just to try to forget -
his reading voice,
his malignant stare,
the way he mused
one heart was plenty.
I guess I can only
plea for some
respite of rest.
Perhaps one day
this maleficent
memory of mine
will finally come to
terms with our
death.

~ Second-Hand Spouse ~

You reek of
someone else
and I'm trying to
withstand the odour
of ardour
but this betrayal
won't sit right
in my mouth.
I've tried replacing
your unripe
repentance with
divorcees, but
these twilight
rendezvous
keep dancing South.
You tell me I'm
a westward wife,
a second-hand spouse,
but I'm not the one
trampling torpedoes
over your health.
You know, this
treason will give
me a clobbered
sense of self.
If only I could also be
cherished by
someone else…

~ Ailing Autumn ~

We gather fallen leaves
pretending these
crisp tendrils
were not us
last week,
teething on moss-bitten
midwinter fights.
I play *Red* in the Chevy
and you remark
love like that must
feel blood-gushing,
but I don't remember
the last time you
haunted us to life.
I think perhaps
I should batter your
bullshit, your
crater-chunking curses,
your frostbitten lies.
Maybe then I'll
start to encompass
the deity
who was once
so coruscating...
So worldly...
So *wise*...

~ You Could Never Love A Lacerated Girl ~

I think I'll just
lay down
until the world stops,
resume crunching
your ribs between
my teeth.
You carried her
cadaver when the
eclipse came,
lay posies by her
pallid feet.
You could never
love a lacerated girl,
whine during her
wilting, weave petals
atop her ailment sheet.
I guess I'm just the
curse that crevices
your heart to clubs,
melted this queen
devoid of
matrimony.
I guess I'm just the
injury that
begged you watch me
burnout and
bleed.
What a catastrophic
legacy to leave.
What a fatal frailty

to believe.
I guess *I'm* the reason
you could never
cradle
me.

~ You're Not A Hot Commodity, Babe ~

I dream of you
in waves,
ivy creeping upon
my pores,
cyanide spilling
onto this
crusted tongue.
Why have I waited
decades to
post these
elegies to your door,
risk a rejection
that could
incapacitate
crooning
lungs?
It's not as though you're
some *hot commodity*.
You're not even
tepid
most dusks at the
drive-in, flailing away
this festering fun.
Why, for you,
would I still come
undone?
This jovial
Juliet

*doesn't quite
know when to run...*

~ *Python* ~

Cut my throat
before you leave.
Please.
Tease my taste buds
with viper
vermillion.
The only devotion
I ever
plagued from your
throbbing carcass
was stained
cerulean.
You blame my
boredom for
'*encouraging* this',
for manifesting
these festering
frictions.
Our adoration
expired in a
butchery
because barbarity
bled into your
rage-fed addiction.

~ Fifteen-Karat Reality ~

Crystal skies
burn in the recesses
of my mind
as I attempt to process
your ailing anarchy.
How can a guy
who sputters
up spiders
ever be the scab picker
of sanctity?
Perhaps I've been
coughing up
your cobwebs,
trying to manifest
a fifteen-karat
reality.
At least I can admit
I was starry-eye
soaked
in your sultry
calamity.

~ Feed (I Always Knew You Would) ~

That's the way
love goes -
being left on read,
regurgitating the tar
of unrequited
empathy.
How many dawns
will I have to
bleed,
soaked in the
shallows of these
aspartic dreams?
I'm tying my
sanity
to these rotten reeds,
decapitated from
sullied
seams.
How many more
nights will I continue
to seethe, teethe
the leaking heart
you adorned to
my sleeve?
How many
of my realities
will you grasp
through
gluttonous

greed?
On how many of
my limbs
would you like
to
feed?

~ Devilish Doting ~

In the shallow of
the forest, I clutch
the remnants of
myself.
The girl paraplegic
down by the river
bend, carcass pooling
by the foaming
mouth.
How did I cripple
here and why did you
slay me so?
The sensual scripts
you sewed vowed
me everlasting
tomorrows.
I never thought I'd
exhume my own
cadaver, curse as the
ripples
ravaged my corroding.
Bones brittle beneath
the mossy bend,
algae
frothing upon my
clothing.
I wish you nothing but
sonorous perdition.
I want you to shudder
how hope is

massacred.
After all, it was always
your insecurity
that meshed doting
manacled.

~ Choking Chest-Strings ~

Will you still
kiss my scars
even though we're
light years apart?
Will you still
heave hope
onto my chest-strings
with your edible
abstract art?
Sometimes I wish
we could chew
the elated embers of
our phosphorescent
start.
If only our
headstrong
huntress
history
wasn't stapled
to my forlorn,
faltering
heart.

~ Fermented Abyss ~

Will you come back
if I say please?
Knock on this cranium
of mine with
reinvention and an
apology?
Explore my tattered
psyche with those
dew-dripping keys?
Decode why these
smudged dusks are
chewing the better
of me.
I guess I always foresaw
you'd maul and
leave.
This cyclical cyclone
has been brewing for
weeks.
I guess it all impeded
as a bit of a tease.
Now I'm gazing into
a fermented abyss from
wreckage-slathered peaks…

~ Go To Hell ~

I betrayed myself
for a slice of your
love
and now I'm
haemorrhaging
desperation.
I clung onto your
threadbare words
and segmented
a hefty ration.
This dermis
was drenched
in clotted icing as
you massacred my
elation.
I guess my chest
grieved the most
when you
liquidated your
senseless
declaration.

~ Lychee Limbs ~

Take her home,
be her home.
What's it to me?
You erected a fortress
for these lychee
limbs
and then dubbed her
your majesty.
I guess I'm the
disposable damsel,
the monarch of
honed hyperbole.
You chewed on her
dull disposition
like she was your
cryptic fantasy.
Perhaps this absence
is getting the better
of me -
This gaping wound,
these loose guts,
on display for amputee.
Or maybe I'm certain
this was the divinest
dreamscape,
the grandest *something*
to ravish this
nobody.
Then again, I guess I'll
have to coruscate

with this crooked Gemini,
these predictions that
munch me up and
ingurgitate the key.
Once I've finally accepted
my feral fate,
I can plummet into
Syncope.
I always *knew* you'd be
the end of
me.

~ Stop Composing Soliloquies. I Am Not Poetry. ~

My chest
is chewing on the
crust of calamity,
and I am falling
victim to char.
I can feel myself
going under whilst
there is an air
of tribulation
crocheting
calloused
scars.
Why did you have to
drag me to
Atlantis, leave
my skin puffed
and saggy?
Why did you ever
lift me to the ether,
then compost
my crooked body?
If there is
something to learn
here, I guess it's
that beasts come
in beautiful form,
gliding atop the
peaks of praise,

composing soliloquies
galore.
Try me, then.
Go on – press my
corpse for the truth...
The proof...
The timeless scoop.
This cadaver will
sting forever,
breathe pestilence,
breed recklessly,
because of *you*.

~ Traitor ~

I'm still brushing
the pallid
off my face,
and obliterating
the comets that
blitzed us to space,
because you
shred your skin that
you extolled me,
and laughed as they
dragged
me
away...

~ Detonation Days ~

My heart looks
pretty in your hands,
all before you start
compressing
your bones together
fissuring
internal
ERUPTION.
My soul looks
bulletproof
until you detonate
it beneath your
unchaste gaze.
I never thought
I'd have to
apologise to a
predator
for causing dinner
party disruptions,
dowsing my pores in
self-preservation just
to cleanse my
sentience from these
flames.
I guess you're not the
same guy who
offered that
coy introduction,
blushed as he
recited his name.

I guess you're just
a beast who teethes
on my flesh and
plays macabre
party games.
Oh how I wish I
never loved you
this way...

~ Little Girl Lost ~

I sob centuries
but I am so
productive,
and isn't that
exactly what a
good girl
should be?
I've been slow dancing
with the laundry
and writing my poems
on kitchen cloth.
I've been hiding
beneath the four-poster
and playing
little
girl
lost.
Oh what I'd give to
leave this mansion
crawling with cobwebs,
drenched in its own
crucifixion.
Oh what I'd give
to have this feeble
fable
be a work of
fiction.
So I'll keep penning
works of art
on my arm.

Rewriting my future
on my palm.
And then I'll meander
into the West woods.
And then I'll take
to the ether
and run...

~ Phosphorescent Pedestal ~

I have endless problems
and you're the reason
for *all* of them…
The bracken bones
fraying the crust
of my reinvention.
How am I supposed to
crush ceilings
when you're reminding
me you're
always
on
top,
watching my wilting
from a phosphorescent
pedestal,
injecting incandescence
into your own
chuckles,
your own sarcastic
remarks,
your jilted
cross-stitched lips?
Anyone would think
we were once the
luminescence
coruscating
like a green light
upon the curling waters
of the Atlantic.

Little do they know,
we're emigrating seas,
arch-nemesis archetypes,
two corpses
crouching in their own
power complexes.
Little do they know,
only one of us
will make it
out
alive.

~ Enkindling Catastrophe ~

They say that 'to write'
is to purge your
rage on a parchment,
to pen your seething
on a script.
But what do you do
when nothing seems
to ease the
vexation?
What reality do you
ingurgitate
when
no revenge
seems quite fitting enough?
I guess there is only
so much purging
you can seek from
soul-scathing,
mind-fracturing,
heart-hastening.
I guess there is only
so much a vigilante
can scour the moors
of inhospitableness
and yearn to
enkindle catastrophe.

~ I'm Just A Girl Glued To Guttering ~

I've been rotting
in the basement
of your adoration
and the window
in here is wedged shut
and blacked-out
and the rafters are
dilapidated
like the croaking stairs
that lead to the
semi-detached we've
rented in the
French Alps.
I've always wanted to
taste glaciation
and lick the sherbet
off the peaks
on the other side
of this
guttered ribcage.
But *here I am,*
reading my death
sentence in the hollow
crust of your chest,
begging for
mercurial mercy.
This is no sort
of life for a maiden
who regurgitates
a lido of loose love.

A girl who is glued
to guttering.
A sinner who is
magnetised to a
molten existence.
I guess I'll just expire
here, then, in this
hatchet of a holiday
house,
starve in spite
and plummet
parched from self-pity.
I guess I'll just
push myself into
my own
dampening
demise.

~ Torpedo Tongue ~

I still recall your
peppermint kisses
saluting my curves
with divine chimeras.
I still remember those
winters by the
hoarse firelight,
cushioned by your
state of grace.
I didn't think you'd ever
leave me in a
tilted place.
What a fucking lie
it is that you need
sanctified
space.
You're just a torrid
case, 'babe'.
Go and slumber
in
hate.

~ Hungry Apparition ~

I gaze at
geometric ceilings,
waiting for the hypnosis
to subside.
It seems I'm still
embering
into existentialism
with your ghost
perched
by my side.

~ *I'm Just A Horror Story* ~

I wish you could see
I am not the
enemy
here.
I do not hold
your heathens in an
hourglass,
I do not whittle
your whispers
into
warfare.
Don't encase my
intentions.
I'm just a
jilted lover.
You carved
your own curses
and slay
my gut
bare.

~ *Your Dirtiest Work* ~

What would it take
to make this work?
We're barren as
carved
bloodstreams,
tongues
mottled
from
tepid
thirst.
Why do you always
have to put dying first,
like we're both in
catacombs
rescinding
beneath sodden dirt?
You tie thorns
around my torso,
then query if I'm hurt.
I don't know which
shadow of massacre
is the whittled
and worst.
Do you even know
how to clamber curt?
This hexed devotion
cascades like a
curse.
Go on, go back to
putting

you
first.
It always was
your dirtiest work.

~ Execution Tactics ~

You are obsidian.
I press my palm
into you and
disintegrate into the
ether.
I wish I could say
this self-combustion
at least soothed
my soul
but I'm here
ghosting the tarnished
moors of your love
like a Kathy
no Heathcliff would
ever want to know.
You toss
Chinese throwing stars
at my memory
like I was just a
mistress to you
but we both know
nobody ever survived
your execution
tactics so long.
So call me an
ancient curse, claim
I am an unhinged woman,
but *don't you dare*
say you weren't
once hexed

by my
excruciation.

~ Status Quo Spinner ~

Can we talk over dinner?
That way you
can't
ignore
me.
You moan I'm getting
thinner.
You don't want a
wife
ageing
scrawny.
I told my parents
you're a sinner,
but my god they didn't
believe me.
You're a status quo
spinner, a warped
wasteland of reality.
My innards crave for you
to stop undermining
my divinity.
I've had to snip the
umbilical cord
of my dreams, all
for your charred
cavernous
calamity.
I hope one day
you never remember
me.

I hope one lifetime
I can conceal these
serrated screams...

~ Leave Me For The Wolf Pack ~

I am a ghost orchid.
A translucent bloom.
I'd say you still
bled bullets for me,
if you didn't forget
I was in the room.
I'm the camouflage
elephant.
I'm not really there.
Perhaps that's why
the petunias
on our epitaph
lay brittle and bare.
I mourn those library
dates, fissured
Polaroids in plush
frames.
I've never laid my
yearning down
over the tether
of your Gargantuan
games.
So catch me
if I fall, or discard
my devotion
for the wolf pack.
Whether you clutch
my cadaver or not,
my livelihood is

never
coming
back.

~ Trimmed And Teething ~

Spilled Jack Daniels
and midnight rants.
Torn user manuals
and intoxicated dance.
We're like
the uncultured caricatures
your friends
tell you about,
a couple still
trimming and teething,
finding their own
psyches every dawn
in the drought.
I don't know how we
became like this,
a union of
twenty-somethings
who dollop
tulips over trauma
and epitaphs
over epiphanies.
Did I taste teenage
ruin first again
or did you?
All this sodden red
stops me regurgitating
our histories.
Our intentions
have now
embraced

their tombs.
I don't know who'll
taste trauma the
most bruised.
I wonder if
either of us
will even make it
to June...

~ Adulthood Is A Decaying Animal ~

Adulthood is a
decaying animal,
strewn across the 405,
guts kissing
hot Earth.
I didn't mean to
grind the thing,
splay its organs
across central LA.
Would you be
disgusted if I
admitted I chuckled
my chest raw?
Perhaps soon
I'll be the one
slaughtered
on the freeway.

~ Hungry Abattoir ~

*A poem a day
keeps the
transgression away,*
or so you say.
But how is me
writing about this
hungry abattoir
going to
settle
this blame,
bleed you tame,
dowse your
Devil's clutch
in shame?
After all these
cursives, these
couplets, these
curses,
this massacre still
mutilates
the same.
*Don't you know
this self-infliction
is now ingrained?*

~ Tortured Poet ~

Perhaps I am a
tortured poet.
Let's pretend I am
a cityscape – a dense,
doting suburb,
a social pariah with
a neighbourhood
of manuscripts.
Let's pretend I do
not have a paperweight
acting as a skyscraper
to a single crumple
of wood pulp.
Maybe one day
I will flutter
into
notoriety...
Until then, I guess
I will keep penning
this loose
insanity,
pressing
plagues
Until then, I guess I
will keep
searing
sonnets
onto
these
scripts,

hoping my cranium
will not
come
undone.

~ Kingdom Of Lies ~

I siphoned star-dew
from your kingdom
of lies,
slathered your carcass
in tiled deception,
and preached for
a new dawn.
How many times should
a deity have to
collapse on her
knobbly knees
and press her
palms into pacifism?
How many times
should she have to
b l u d g e o n
to be heard?
I want to puke
every time you place
those plagued paws
on my skin,
I want to
regurgitate
arsenic upon you
every time
you dance with
another damsel.
Come on, why
can't I just be
h e a r d?

S e e n?
W a n t e d?
I guess this delectable
dawn has
swallowed its
permanence
before I've had a
chance to snatch it
in my greedy grip.
I guess this
palatable start
is hiding in the
recesses of
non-existence.
I guess I'll just
jester here
and
drown.

~ Shrill And Silent ~

I have a jar
full of tears,
and you have a chest
dowsed in resentment.
Who knew dinner fights
and sleepless nights
would thieve our
short-lived
atonement?
You've bludgeoned
every ounce of magic
from our once-curated
sentiment.
Now every room in
this house is
shrill with silence.

~ Malting Melancholy ~

So just pull the trigger
and watch my innards
gleam golden on the
kitchen countertop.
Go on, press your
perspiring index
upon that extermination
entity, watch my
resting corpse
rot.
There is no way
either of us
are going to
scramble out of
this shambles
alive, so why
not just slay
me shamefully,
let the heathen
in my hubris
just
die?
After all, you won't
be able to plead
for that ocean-view
if you're not
shaken to survive.
Yet here I am,
waiting for the wilting
to come,

apprehending metallic
plutonium
pelting my lungs.
Do you really think
I'm malting melancholy
here just for fun?
*If only I could ravage
your 'righteousness'
and run...*

~ Groundhog Years ~

I'm penning poems
out of tears
and reaping
grit atop these
groundhog years.
If only I could
stomach these
festering fears,
out-cog Father Time
of his gears...
I might even
disappear,
spiral my cadaver
from this sphere.
Can't a girl
revere?

~ I Exhale The Underworld ~

I'm not a saint,
but Charon has not
ferried me through
to Hades' place either.
I exhale the
Underworld, a halo
and a pitchfork
on each shoulder.
A girl really needs
to purge her
lividity
sometimes, slam
her skull against
a burnished release.
What a shame
this constant
reposing in mood,
in thought, in *self*,
fissures me
paraplegic and
deceased.

~ Pestilent Paramour ~

This heart is a morgue,
melting masochism
at its core.
You keep going
in for a gorge,
pressing me for more.
How can I give my
all to a man
who doesn't
inhale human lore?
A barbarian wasn't
the long-lasting paramour
I was looking for...

~ *Grimoire Of Eternal Doom* ~

Smithereens of me
are smeared along
Sacramento and
still you
suction salt
from my wounds.
How was I ever
supposed to
reinvent myself
whilst your woes
were weaved
around my womb.
How does a girl
bypass the grimoire
of eternal doom?
I guess I was always
erected
to be
your
tomb.

~ I Need You To Scorch ~

Therapy is not enough.
I need you to *suffer*.
Combust into fissured flakes
and become dowsed
in twilight until it feasts
on your fur.
Therapy is not enough.
I need you to *scorch*.

~ *Ghosted* ~

The living scare
me more than the dead,
ailing actions
ambling around in
my head.
How can a guy devour
stalk season
with his lover,
then put his devotion
to bed?
Love is the craziest
word I ever said.
It's unhinged how
much a girl
can burgeon
once
she's
bled.

~ Drifting Into Delusion ~

We are studded
with delicate words
and yet no amount of
embellishment
can stop the
past
from slashing us
into diamanté shards
and eclipsing our facade.
We once committed
espionage of emotion
but now the only
contrivance about us that
speaks soothing
are our appetites for
one another's ventricles,
our craving for
one another's
curling chests.
So keep embossing us
with opals,
keep adorning us in
topaz.
We'll drift into
delusion either way.

~ Heart Attack ~

I'm too pretty
to be suffering like this,
falling victim to
the
bounties you scrape
atop my severed skull,
sweeping damnation
off my skin.
I'm too divine to be
waiting by the phone
for you
to
never
call
back.
I'm too much of a catch
to be chasing
Colossus.
Love, no matter
how hard you try,
you won't
grant me a
heart attack.

~ Dead Dreamscape ~

When you said you'd
leave me with a part
of your heart,
I had no clue you'd
abscond me to the
core -
the fleshy, meaty
habitat of hives
that berated me
like a sore.
After those luminary
dawns and those
transient, crescent-stained
midnights, I had no
idea you'd dispose
of this dead dreamscape
at my door.
A severed artery
wasn't exactly what
I was bleeding for.

~ What If The Grief Comes In Stages? ~

Words tumble from
florets, carving
calligraphy on
crusted pages.
What if this literature
is making me less
depressed – a
divine being to
coruscate through
the ages?
I've spent my days
chewing on led
but what if the grief
comes in stages?
And what if these
vowels wipe away
the rest, erupt plush
vivacity onto my
forlorn phases?

~ Talk Of The Town ~

We're decomposing
on a burning terrace
and there is nothing
I can do to
extinguish
this humiliation.
Wine Mums whisper
about the town
with arsenic tongues,
spurting fables
about our torrid
situation.
I've tried to hex
this dying love
but nothing I mouth
is channelling our
incantation.
I guess we'll just
incinerate here, then,
with bloody cysts,
igniting in puddles
of our scorched elation.

I dreamt you ate
my cartilage
and spat me atop
the curling
moors.
So much for
*'You know I
love you'* and
mundane
mauling wars.
I had a premonition
my innards were
spewed all over
our kitchen floor.
Now, love.
Really.
What are we
crusading for?

~ Try Me. I Dare You. ~

You're sending me
messages from
mercury
but I remark I'm
only part
Venus.
I do not vibe
with this toxic
masculinity, this
varicose vanity,
this desire to be
fleek and famous.
I could scream
skyscrapers from my
mottled tongue
and you'd still
dub women
shameless.
One more snigger
and I'll dowse you
in my
dauntless.

You puke up my
praise and feed on
your own putrefying.
Don't challenge me, love.
I'm the Queen of
gorging on grief, the
high-priestess of
self-crucifying.

~ Until We Rot ~

Depicting this blemished
bite in rhyme, we
incinerate one another
to pass the time.
How do we resolve the
dynamite that
dances in the place of our
mutual acclaim?
How do we stop
weaving war into our
words and strap
civility to our brains?
We've tried abandoning
this apparition
but we just
can't
stop.
I guess we'll keep swinging
at this core, then,
until we *rot*.

~ Idle Lips ~

We're harboured
in hydrochloride.
You've injected
iodine into my irises.
Am I in coalition
with your sapient spies?
Froth is free-flowing
out of my sinuses.
The killer in me
just wants to survive.
I'm hexing atop your
skull
viper-shawled viruses.
There's no way
we're making our way
out of this alive.
The night-borne mares
are slipping from
idle
lips.

~ Decadent Lie ~

It begins with a *no,*
and ends in
goodbye.
A grand entrance
hand-held by
a battle cry.
There's no such
authenticity in
telling a decadent lie.
I just end up
catastrophising
the reasons *why...*

~ Unchaste Province ~

I'm looking to
get lost
in my hatred
of you.
I'm seeking to flutter
into fidelity
with my repulsion
of your
shallow-drowning
antics, your intoxicated
cutlery-throwing skills,
your accuracy at
tossing throwing stars
into my anatomical
galaxy.
I'm trying to
dive into the dollops
of disgust at
your endurance.
Your unchaste
province
is no longer the
homeland
for me.

~ Mum Says... ~

When love turns lonely,
let it go.
Watch it bite the ether
and evanesce
to snow.
Bestow upon your
lonely
a midnight glow.
Shelf your sorrow.
Permit the tendrils
free-flow.

~ This Is No Horror Story ~

Ochre-painted tree lines
tip like willows
atop my skull.
I traipse through
this verdant expanse,
searching for someplace
to lull.
Isn't it funny how
every wilted wood
is depicted in a
horror story.
To flee from one's
own domestication
prevents the
broadest
gut of gory.
I think I'll
wander here
for a while,
frost my footing
in this iridescent
brush.
Soak into slumber
in rattan reeves,
escape from
suburban slush.
Just wake me,
please, when my
returning is due.
I'll pick myself up

from wanderlust
and
let
eternal
fear
brew.
Drifting into dense
wasteland makes
you evolve anew.
Mutes the martyrdom.
Plucks the misery.
Who knew?

~ Pink Haze ~

I'm waiting for a
new dusk -
one that doesn't
embellish my
dermis in
mercury.
Perhaps I'm
internally weaving
some sort of
pink haze, a
burnished bleeding
of Hermes.
All I want is to
clutch my bones,
embrace the
essence of home,
repress my
macabre
backstory.
I just need to
chomp on this
cataclysm and
crunch
glory.

~ Tectonic Girl ~

I am harder than
a headstone.
Bestial as a blade.
I'm ungluing myself
from the gutter.
Slashing this shallow
grave.
I'm dancing atop the
dumping ground.
From heterochromia
I was made.
Manacle me, if you dare.
I'll betroth
tectonic waves.

~ That Final Girl Feeling ~

Would we survive
in a gory movie?
Slash the syrup from
each other's chests?
We'd be Stu and Billy,
glued to macabre duty.
And, as for the final girl,
I'd butcher the best.

~ Tourniquet Tongue ~

You ask me to
down a shot of truth
but if I am to chug
and regurgitate anything
it will be the fables
you have been foaming
from your
tourniquet
tongue.
Trust me, I'm appending
my cerebrum to
this ending.
I'm finally going to be
someone.

~ Remains ~

I'm digging up the
remains of this
artlessness, plunging
my shovel into the
palette you thieved
from my ashen skull.
I don't quite
understand how
a guy can cradle
the lore of Colossus,
ooze gouache and yet
glimmer so dull.
My stomach stirs,
this soil fissures
and I bite my tongue
just to watch colour
revolt against
your wall.
Snapping this memory
into cartilage,
I rebirth the plot with
ghost orchids,
reminding myself
I can again
feel
full.

~ Coming Alive ~

The burnt moon
kissed my lips gently,
left me
leaking
mercury.
The planets cradled
my plushness,
injected my bloodstream
with star-dew.
I lift my loins
towards the sun,
let her claw my
yearning, hail
me Hercules.
I'll praise these
seasons, these
lotus petals,
and let this triumph
tease me from
my
tomb.

~ Almighty ~

The divine feminine
is woven into
my hair,
embroidered into
my ribcage,
and meshed into my
psyche.
Persephone's lore...
Atlas' assertion...
I will not let these
bold manifestos
escape me.
I was raised to
be
almighty.

~ Darling ~

I want someone to
love me different
but these fish
gulp down mundanity
like a fine delicacy.
Perhaps the only one
who can adore me
like a darling is
the one who scales
foam at high tide.
Perhaps the only
girl who can kiss
my spirit is
me.

Ellie Sparks is a Creative Writing graduate from the University of Winchester. She adores writing poetry in her free time, listening to Paramore and Taylor Swift at an ear-bleeding volume, and playing with her two cats, Socks and Slippers. She hopes to write many more young adult poetry collections and is excited about producing much more work. She can be found via Instagram at @justtryingtobeoriginal.

Printed in Great Britain
by Amazon

50a79734-337a-4aeb-83a6-3a87fa03d0f9R02